Out of the Blue

WALLACE EDWARDS

Out of
the Blue

North Winds Press
An Imprint of Scholastic Canada Ltd.

The art for this book was created with pencil, watercolour and gouache.

Library and Archives Canada Cataloguing in Publication

Edwards, Wallace, author, illustrator
Out of the blue / Wallace Edwards.

ISBN 978-1-4431-4872-6 (hardcover)

I. Title.

PS8559.D88O87 2018   jC813'.6   C2018-901355-9

www.scholastic.ca

6 5 4 3 2 1   Printed in Malaysia 108   18 19 20 21 22

To Katie, my love.

And to Gordon, George, Leonie, Chase, Miles, Genevieve, Abigail, Sage, Harriet and Stella.

Ernest was flying his kite when it got stuck in a tree.

He tried and tried . . .

. . . but he could not get it down on his own.

While Ernest sat missing his kite, there was a
sudden loud noise in the sky.

What could it be? Was there danger? Did someone need help?

Ernest was tired and scared but his need to know pushed him on.

When he saw what had fallen, Ernest
still did not understand.

He sensed he wasn't alone.

A MONSTER! DANGER!
RUN AWAY!

But maybe the stranger wasn't as horrible as Ernest first feared.

Ernest and the creature sat down and stared at each other.

And Ernest understood!

His friend needed help.

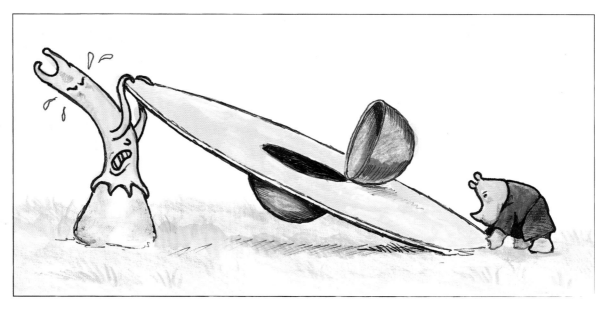

And when his new friend asked what he could do in return, Ernest remembered that he needed some help too.

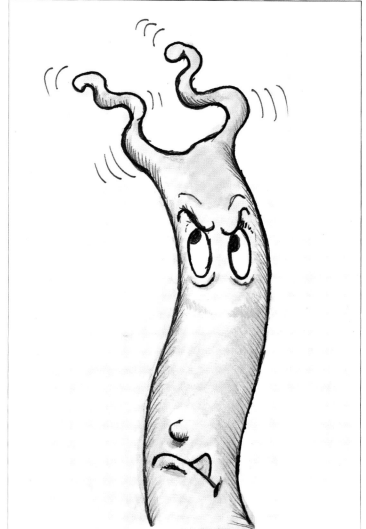

Too soon, it was time to say goodbye.

Though they said it in different ways, they each knew what the other meant:

Thank you!

And there were no more
monsters, only friends.